Sidekicks

Sidekicks
THE CANDY MAN COMETH

by Dan Danko and Tom Mason

Illustrated by Barry Gott

LITTLE, BROWN AND COMPANY

New York ⤙ Boston

3 3187 00209 1490

Text copyright © 2004 by MainBrain Productions
Illustrations copyright © 2004 by Barry Gott

Little, Brown and Company

Time Warner Book Group
1271 Avenue of the Americas, New York, NY 10020
Visit our Web site at www.lb-kids.com

First Edition

Library of Congress Cataloging-in-Publication Data
Danko, Dan.
The Candy Man cometh / by Dan Danko and Tom Mason ;
illustrated by Barry Gott. — 1st ed.
p. cm. — (Sidekicks ; 4)
Summary: Speedy and the other sidekicks help out when the
League of Big Justice faces its stickiest, most chocolatey
supervillain yet — the Candy Man, who is determined to rot
the world's teeth one cavity at a time.
ISBN 0-316-73428-4
[1. Heroes — Fiction. 2. Adventure and adventurers — Fiction.
3. Humorous stories.] I. Mason, Tom. II. Gott, Barry, ill. III. Title.
PZ7.D2285Can 2004
[Fic] — dc22   2003026599

10 9 8 7 6 5 4 3 2 1
LAKE

Printed in the United States of America

The text for this book was set in Bookman,
and the display type is Bernhard Gothic Heavy Italic.
Book design by Billy Kelly

To Ginger, the best sidekick in the world
(except for Boy-in-the-Plastic-Bubble Boy)
— Dan

To Yaela, Who Lets Me
Do This for a Living!
— Tom

Chapter One
Bonding with Pumpkin Pete

"What was your last sidekick like?" I asked Pumpkin Pete.

Pumpkin Pete shook his big, fat, orange pumpkin head. "Oh . . . he was a real pain in the you-know-what."

"Really?"

"Oh, yeah," Pete snorted. "All that kid did was complain, complain, complain."

"About what?" I asked.

"Pfft. Try everything. From the moment that kid put the first coat of wax on the Pumpkin-mobile to the day he ironed my last Super Shirt of Pumpkinness, all that kid did was whine."

"But, like, what about?"

"Oh, I don't know, really," Pete answered. "He wanted me to teach him stuff and help him learn things. Always begging for me to tell him about the Mysterious Ways of the Pumpkin and blah, blah, blah. As if just *anyone* could be allowed into the Obscure Inner Circle of the Pumpkin." Pete shook his head again.

"Who *is* allowed in the Obscure Inner Circle of the Pumpkin?" I asked.

"Anyone with a pumpkin for a head. And if you ask me, the bigger, the fatter, and the oranger, the better," Pete replied. "Or is it 'orangier'?"

"But Pete, *you're* the only one in the world with a pumpkin for a head," I reminded him.

"Yeah, I know. The Inner Circle meetings are real dull. That's why I never go. But I'll tell you this much, my life got a whole lot easier the day I kicked that kid to the curb," Pete said.

"Wow. What happened?"

"I was just driving along and the kid was, like, 'Blah blah blah blah! Whine whine whine.' So I just pulled over the Pumpkinmobile and kicked him out!" Pete explained.

All of this was suddenly sounding familiar. "What kind of powers did he have?" I asked.

Pete wrinkled his nose and thought for a moment. "He . . . uh . . . he had the power to give me a headache. I really don't remember. I never talked to him much."

"Why not?" I prodded.

"Because if I said something to him, then he'd probably say something back to me, and then I'd probably have to answer and a conversation might break out," Pete said in a condescending tone, as if he were explaining the obvious. He stopped and scratched his hollow pumpkin skull. "What was his name again? It was something like Spotty or Spuddy."

"Speedy?" I asked, realizing that my suspicions were correct.

"Yeah! That's it!" Pete excitedly shook a finger. "Man, am I glad that kid's gone."

"Uh . . . Pete," I said, "*I'm* Speedy."

"WHAT!? I thought I kicked you out of the Pumpkinmobile an hour ago!" Pete hit the brakes.

As I stood on the curb and watched Pumpkin Pete zoom away in the Pumpkinmobile, I couldn't help but wonder if this was some kind of test. You know, drop your sidekick-in-training in the middle of nowhere and see how long it takes him to get home.

But then I remembered the last time Pete did this. Man, it took me days to get home from Pluto, and boy was it cold! My parents were so upset when I finally got back to Earth.

I still remember that whole stupid conversation. . . .

CHAPTER ONE-AND-A-HALF
That Whole Stupid Conversation

"I don't care if you did stop the Geduldig invasion fleet at Pluto! The next time you're planning on leaving the solar system, you darn well better call home to get permission first!" my mom scolded when I came home.

"Technically, I didn't leave the solar sys —" I didn't finish the sentence. My mom gave me The Look. Anyone who says parents don't have super powers has never experienced The Look. It can see through closed doors, it can spot a lie a mile away, and it can silence you faster than Captain Haggis on the bagpipes. Actually, Captain Haggis on the bagpipes doesn't silence you so much as make you wish *he* were silent.

"And really, son," my dad joined in, "it's at times like this that I really don't think being a superhero sidekick is such a good idea. Your mother and I were worried sick. Put yourself in our shoes, son. We don't know if you're fighting alien invasions on Pluto or hanging over some mad scientist's mutated leech pit."

"I know, Dad. I'm sorry. It's just that sometimes when I'm saving the world and all, I don't really have time to call home."

"Your brother *always* has time to call home no matter how busy *he* is!" Mom chided.

"But Mom! Brad's just a florist! He doesn't have to punch evil in the face!" I said.

"How would you know? Have you ever had to protect a strawberry plant from a pill bug? Have you?" my mom asked.

"No . . . but I did defeat the giant robot that was trying to —"

"Look, son," my dad said, "we're not trying to be hard on you. It's just that being a superhero sidekick doesn't mean you can forget about your other responsibilities. Now I know you saved the planet from being 'enslaved' by evil Geduldig overlords and ensured that your mother and I can peacefully live out the rest of our lives without the fear of working in their salt mines until we die of starvation, but even though you were the lone reason we averted an 'interstellar war' that would've resulted in the 'deaths of millions of innocent lives,' I'm still going to have to revoke your TV and phone privileges for two weeks."

"Fine!" I said, throwing my arms up in the air. "Next time I'll just let the alien hordes win!"

"Now who would you really be hurting if you did that? Hmmm?" my dad asked. "I think . . . you."

I threw down my sidekick goggles and raced up to my room. About ten minutes later there was a knock on the door.

It was my dad.

"It's tough being a sidekick, huh?" he asked.

"Not for the other sidekicks," I replied. "I mean, between Pumpkin Pete and you and Mom . . ."

"Let me tell you, it's pretty tough being a parent, too. Most parents just have to worry about their kids getting into trouble or making bad decisions . . . but I have to worry about my son being disintegrated."

Ever since Pete accidentally fired the League of Big Justice's Disintegration Ray of Zappiness and nearly hit me, I swear, Dad just won't let it go.

"I know, Dad, but you and Mom said you'd support me!"

"That we did, but we never said we wouldn't *worry* about you. Almost every day that I watch you head off to the League of Big Justice, I can't help but think I made a mistake."

"So you don't want me to be a sidekick? You'd be so proud if I was just Junior Assistant Florist, wouldn't you?!"

"Some days . . . yes."

I couldn't believe it! He'd rather I was a florist than a superhero? For a second I hoped that my parents had been replaced by evil clones and this was just one small cog in some giant evil plot to destroy the League of Big Justice and the Sidekicks. Sure! Replace all of their parents with evil clones who would tell them they'd rather they were florists than superheroes, and suddenly the entire League of Big Justice calls it quits and opens one giant flower shop.

Boy, would evil laugh on *that* day. And it wouldn't just be because King Justice was selling daisies.

"You think I love all this, too?" I grumbled. "It totally sucks that I can't tell anyone I have super powers. Do you know how popular I'd be?"

"We all have to give something up in our lives, son. Some more than others . . ."

We all have to give something up? I thought to myself. Yeah. Right. What'd Dad ever have to give up? He's an accountant, for gosh sakes! He'll never understand. No one does. Being my age can really suck. Living a secret life and lying to my friends and getting grief from my parents about it *always* sucks.

And nearly getting devoured by mutant leeches? I don't *even* want to tell you how much *that* sucks! Because . . . uh . . . see . . . leeches, they suck.

My life used to be normal. The only lecture I ever got from my dad was about being nicer to my mom and not trying to break the parental-lock passwords on their Internet account. But that was before the day I ran at 27 miles per hour into a wall. I woke up an hour later and realized two very important things:

IMPORTANT THING #1
Running into a wall at 27 miles
per hour really, really hurts.

IMPORTANT THING #2
I, Guy Martin, had super powers.

I also learned that the one thing more important than seeing how fast I could run was learning how to stop. So I guess that means I learned three important things that day.

Later on I learned a very important fourth

thing: nearly getting devoured by mutant leeches sucks, but I think I already told you that.

But everything changed that day. Rather than having an awesome ability that would make me the most popular person in school, it became an awesome secret — something I had to hide from everyone. I never knew being a superhero would be such a burden.

I mean, forget about that fact that some nut or alien was always trying to kill you, and just think about how rotten it would be knowing that you might be the *only* thing standing between Earth's survival and eternal enslavement in the salt mines of Geduldigopia.

And let me tell you, the weather on Geduldigopia is totally rotten!

That's a lot for a kid to take in!

Don't get me wrong. I love being a sidekick. Sure, my League of Big Justice superhero sponsor, Pumpkin Pete is . . . well . . . not your traditional hero. And I'm not just saying that because he has a big, fat, orange pumpkin for a head. Let's just say he's heroically challenged and leave it at that.

I mean, now I can run more than 100 miles per hour and I get to fight alongside the greatest superhero that ever walked the earth: King

Justice, founder of the League of Big Justice. Well, I don't always fight *alongside* him. More like behind him. The lucky sidekick who gets to fight alongside King Justice is Charisma Kid.

Who, by the way, is a total jerk.

And get this, in his secret identity, Charisma Kid and I go to the same school. His real name is Mandrake Steel.

Who, by the way, is also a total jerk.

Chapter Two
Earlobe Lad Still Can't Fly

"Okay, you sidekicks," Pumpkin Pete said as he paced in front of us, holding his long, viney arms behind his back. "I lost a bet with Captain Haggis, so I'm stuck training you again."

Spice Girl, Boy-in-the-Plastic-Bubble Boy, Boom Boy, Exact Change Kid, Charisma Kid, Earlobe Lad, Spelling Beatrice, and I all stood at attention like we were eight sidekicks who were standing at attention because we were sidekicks and we were standing at attention.

And there were eight of us.

Running at 102 miles per hour, it didn't take me long to race back to the Sidekick Super Clubhouse. Pete had already started this week's training session and, as usual, seemed to have completely forgotten that he'd dropped me off in the middle of downtown only minutes before.

Pumpkin Pete took a step toward Earlobe Lad. Earlobe Lad staggered backward and waved his hands in front of his face. "Don't throw me off the roof again! Please!" he gasped.

Pete's face suddenly brightened. "Oh yeah! You're that kid who can't fly!"

"Yes! Yes! That's me! I *can't* fly!" Earlobe Lad whispered as loudly as he could, doing his best to protect his super-sensitive ears.

Pete scratched his big, fat, orange pumpkin head. "You'd think with ears that big, all you'd have to do is flap 'em a few times and it's ZOOM! into the sky with you!" Pete wiggled Earlobe Lad's enormous earlobe. "You ever try flapping these things?"

Earlobe Lad clutched his big ears and fell into a fetal position. "Why do all of you hate me?" he mumbled.

"We don't hate you," Pete assured him. "We just want you to be a little less worthless in a fight."

A few weeks ago Pumpkin Pete had thrown Earlobe Lad off the top of the Sidekick Super Clubhouse and shouted "Fly! Fly!" The next day,

King Justice, the leader of the League of Big Justice, made a new rule. When it was Pumpkin Pete's turn to train the Sidekicks, he had to do it on the ground, in the League of Big Justice Parking Lot of Big Parking. And far away from sharp objects. And stairs. And no more bombs. Or milk cartons. Apparently the League of Big Justice's insurance bills were high enough without Pete throwing Spandex-wearing teenagers off rooftops.

And it's a long story about the milk cartons, but let's just say it took Boom Boy four months before he could eat cereal without trembling.

You're probably wondering, when does evil attack, and when do I get to punch it in the face? I ask myself that all the time, too.

See, being a sidekick isn't always about being a hero, although there was that one time Captain Haggis called me the "hero o' th' dishwasher." But that was only because I was able to scrub the crusted lamb gravy from his favorite haggis dish. Unfortunately, being a sidekick is more about paying your do's. No, not dues. *Do's.*

At four o'clock, you gotta *do* the laundry. Then after that, you gotta *do* some vacuuming in the Pumpkinmobile, and don't forget to *do* the ironing. That's what Pumpkin Pete considered training me for action. "All the action of making my life just a little easier," he always says to me.

Don't get me wrong, even with the slave labor, I still love being a sidekick. Well, maybe not *love,* exactly, but it's pretty cool to hang out with the world's mightiest superheroes, even if it's just to pick up their dirty laundry. I get to wear an awesome costume and use my super powers. Nothing feels better than using your abilities to help people and maybe make a difference now and then.

Yeah, I guess I have saved the world a few times. Sure, Pumpkin Pete always gets all the credit. "There's only room for one superhero in this photo, and I have a big, fat, orange head. Like a pumpkin!" he'd always say to me when the news crews would rush up after we defeated some villain.

And by "we," of course, I mean me.

But most of all, I knew that if I stuck with it, if I worked really, really hard and proved myself to be a good sidekick, one day when I was older I might be chosen as a member of the League of Big Justice itself! And then *I'd* get my own sidekick to do my laundry!

"Today, we're going to go over a few of the

rules to being a superhero," Pete said as he stepped over Earlobe Lad and continued to pace the line. "There're lots of rules. Lots and lots. I don't know many of them, but I just know there's, like, an encyclopedia full of them."

Spelling Beatrice suddenly perked up. "Did you say encyclopedia?"

Pete ignored her and continued. "If you ever break these rules, you'll be kicked out of the Sidekicks! So remember these rules and follow them as if they were important. Rule #1: Never, never, never tell anyone your real name, even a superhero. You must guard your secret identity as if it were a secret." Pete spun on his heel and stabbed a viney finger at Spice Girl. She jumped back, startled. Suddenly, I could smell a thick garlic scent filling the air. She blushed.

"You," Pete said. "What's your name?"

Spice Girl gave a sigh of relief. "Heather Britney!"

Pete slapped his head with his palm. "You just broke Rule #1! You're outta the Sidekicks!"

"I — mean my name is . . . Jane. Jane . . . Janemansterjones!" Spice Girl corrected herself.

"Jane Janemansterjones?! You just broke Rule #1 again!" Pete shouted.

"You can't kick her out of the Sidekicks!" I protested. "She was just answering your question!"

"Oh, and don't you think evil has brilliant tricks like the one I just pulled? Don't you think an evil genius isn't sitting in his and-or her evil basement *right now,* thinking of evil ways to trick you into revealing your secret identities; identities that should be secret like something you don't want anyone to know!? Their evil plans are big! With lots of arrows and numbers and arrows that point to numbers and arrows that point to arrows and arrows that don't point to numbers and arrows that don't point to *anything* and arrows that . . ."

Boom Boy leaned over to me. "Last time he ranted about bunnies for at least five minutes. Wanna go get a soda?"

Chapter Three
In the Basement of Evil

"I did it! I did it!" the Evil Genius shouted in his basement. He stood before a large blueprint, one that covered an entire eight-by-twelve-foot wall and was filled with equations, schematics, illustrations, numbers, and arrows. Lots and lots of arrows. Lots. And lots.

"I have created the perfect plan to trick those foul superheroes into revealing their secret identities as if they were *not* something they didn't want anyone to know!" He laughed loud and hard, like an evil genius who had just devised the perfect plan to trick superheroes into revealing their secret identities as if they were *not* something they didn't want anyone to know.

"And do you know what the key to my entire plan is, Monkey Boy? Do you?!" the Evil Genius shouted at Monkey Boy.

Monkey Boy swung from the water pipe that ran along the ceiling. He screeched loudly and tugged at the diaper that was around his waist. He dropped to the ground and gently beat his little hairy fists against his forehead.

"Wrong!" the Evil Genius spat at Monkey Boy. "It's the arrows! The pointy, pointy arrows! Pointing at . . . things."

"Darrell!" a voice cried out from upstairs.

The Evil Genius looked at his giant blueprint, inspecting every last inch. He gasped, then took a black marker and drew an arrow tip at the end of a line. "Brilliant," he whispered.

"Darrell!" a voice cried out from upstairs.

The Evil Genius turned from the blueprint and talked to Monkey Boy. "First, we will try this plan on the League of Big Justice. Once I have learned their darkest secrets, it will be mere child's play to defeat them. And then, Monkey Boy, no one will stand between me and my conquest of the earth!"

"Darrell!" a voice cried out from upstairs. "I know you can hear me!"

"What do you want?" the Evil Genius finally yelled back. "I'm busy!"

"Well, you're not too busy to take out the garbage, do you hear me, young man?!"

"I'll do it later!" the Evil Genius yelled back.

"You'll do it *now*!"

The Evil Genius gave Monkey Boy a pleading look, hoping his primate partner would spring into action and stop the meddlesome woman upstairs. Monkey Boy picked a flea out of his fur and ate it.

"Mom! I'm plotting to rule the world!" the Evil Genius yelled up.

"The world will still be there *after* you take out the trash!" the voice yelled back.

"Mooooommmmm!"

"Don't make me come down there!"

The Evil Genius threw down his black marker and stomped toward the basement stairs.

"And that monkey had better be wearing his diaper! I'm tired of cleaning up after that little beast!" the voice called back down.

Monkey Boy screeched loudly and rolled on the ground. He rocked up to his feet, tore off his diaper, and put it on his head like a stinky white hat.

Chapter Four
Evil Doesn't Brush Its Teeth

"Rule #2!" Pete said, after he'd stopped ranting about arrows.

Boom Boy ran up behind me and slipped back into line with a can of Pow! Soda in his hand. He checked his Sidekick Super Watch of Tickiness. "Hey! Hey! Four minutes and fifty-five seconds! Just like boiling an egg!" he bragged, and took a big gulp of his Pow! Soda.

Exact Change Kid's pencil hovered over his notebook, ready to write down the all-important Rule #2.

"No matter how crazy it sounds, no matter how dangerous you think it may be, always, always do what a superhero asks you to do," Pete informed us. "Superheroes know better than you, and the life they may be trying to save just might be their own."

"But, but, what if you don't want to?" Boom Boy asked.

Pete spun around on his heel. "Who said that?" he gasped.

Boom Boy raised his hand . . . and pointed to Exact Change Kid. Exact Change Kid looked up from his notepad, his glasses slightly askew from the zeal with which he wrote.

"Huh?" he said.

Pete took a step toward Exact Change Kid. "So you don't want to do what a superhero tells you to do? What? You too good for the people who save the earth every day like they're just tying their shoelaces?"

The funny thing was, Pete didn't know how to tie his shoelaces.

"That's why the Russians created Velcro!" Pete once said to me as he Velcroed his shoes.

"NASA invented Velcro," I informed him.

"NASA? Is that near Switzerland?"

Pete inched closer to Exact Change Kid and gave him the Pumpkin Eye. "What's your name, Quarter Boy?"

"Uh . . . well . . . actually . . . my name's Exact Change Kid, not Quarter Boy. . . ." Small beads of sweat were starting to form on Exact Change Kid's brow.

"I mean, what's your *real* name? Your parents didn't put 'Quarter Boy' on your birth certificate, did they?" Pete pressed.

Exact Change Kid brightened and was about to answer, but then stopped, remembering Rule #1: Never reveal your secret identity, even to a superhero.

"I'm sorry, sir, but as you taught us with Rule #1, 'Never, never, never tell anyone your real name, even a superhero.'" Exact Change Kid was proud he had passed the test.

"Oh, sure, sure!" Pete replied, and put an arm around Exact Change Kid. "But I'm sure you also remember Rule #2?"

"'Always do what a superhero asks you to do'!" Boom Boy jumped in and gave a knowing wink to Exact Change Kid.

"And right now, a superhero is *asking* you your real name," Pete said. "Unless you're saying that *I'm* not a superhero . . . that I *don't* have all the powers of a pumpkin!"

Small beads of sweat ran down Exact Change

Kid's temple. He looked at his notebook where he had written Rule #1 and #2 and underlined them several times.

After an uncomfortable pause he began, "My name's Myron Stra —"

Pete interrupted Exact Change Kid and slapped him on the back. "You just broke Rule #1! You're outta the Sidekicks!"

"But . . . but . . . ," Exact Change Kid stammered.

"Hey, I don't make the rules, I just enforce them." Pete pointed Exact Change Kid toward the street in front of the League of Big Justice and shooed him along with his hands. Exact Change Kid slumped slightly as he shuffled away.

"That's not fair, Pete!" I protested. "You can't kick him out for breaking Rule #1 when he had to break Rule #1 to follow Rule #2!"

"Whoa! Slow down there, egghead!" Pete chuckled. "Save the algebra for the classroom."

"You can't kick Exact Change Kid and Spice Girl out of the Sidekicks! They were just doing what you told them!" I was waving my arms above my head like it would somehow help convince Pete.

"Are you saying that I made a mistake?" Pete growled.

"No! I'm just saying that maybe you shouldn't kick them out of the Sidekicks for just doing what you said."

"You wanna know what happens when a su-perhero makes a mistake?" Pete snarled.

"Uh . . . no," I answered.

"Well, I'll tell you! Superheroes don't make mistakes! That's why we're *super*heroes! If we made mistakes, then we'd be *not*-so-superheroes, wouldn't we? And that'd make you *not*-so-sidekicks!"

Boom Boy shrugged his shoulders. "Makes sense to me!"

"It's good to hear you admit you can make a mistake." Pete relaxed. "Of course, that means you can never be a superhero, because super-heroes don't *make* mistakes!" Pumpkin Pete spun back to face the rest of us. "And that leads us to Rule #3! Even a superhero can make a mistake!"

Spelling Beatrice shook her head in silent misery. "This is giving me a headache," she said with a sigh.

Chapter Five
"I'm Sad Now"

Spice Girl sat on the curb that ran along the League of Big Justice Parking Lot of Big Parking. She leaned back and supported herself with her palms. She was surprisingly upbeat for having just been kicked out of the Sidekicks. She watched Exact Change Kid shuffle over from the rest of the group and sit down next to her.

"Hey," Exact Change Kid mumbled, and plopped on the curb.

"Hey."

"They kicked me out of the Sidekicks, too." Exact Change Kid let out a long sigh and scratched his head. He flipped open his pocket notebook and reviewed his scribbled writings. *Rule #1:*

Never, never, never tell anyone your real name. Rule #2: Always do what a superhero asks you to do. Exact Change Kid dropped his head into his hands. His notebook fell to the asphalt. "Where did I go wrong?"

"I think when you landed on Park Place," Spice Girl suggested.

"All I've ever wanted was to be a sidekick . . . to use my uncanny powers of exact change to battle the forces of evil." Exact Change Kid reached into his utility belt and pulled out a fistful of coins. He opened his hand and stared at the little heads. "Abe. George. Thomas. And good ol' FDR. I've let you down. I've let all of you down."

"Don't worry so much," Spice Girl assured him. "The last time Peter Pumpkin kicked me out of the Sidekicks, I just went home and watched TV. When I came back the next day, he didn't even remember my name. He called me 'Stinky.'"

"Really?" Exact Change Kid brightened. "You mean there's still a chance I can be a sidekick?"

"No. Probably not this time. I'm just telling you what happened before."

Exact Change Kid deflated like a balloon that was just kicked out of the balloon version of the Sidekicks.

He looked at Spice Girl. An idea drifted into his head. "But . . . I guess on the bright side . . . you and I can spend some time together. Maybe go watch some TV . . ." Exact Change Kid smiled and nudged himself ever so slightly nearer to Spice Girl.

"I'm sad now," she said.

Chapter Six
Evil Eats the Last Fig Newton

Boom Boy sat down next to Earlobe Lad. The two didn't say anything to each other. Usually Boom Boy liked to torment Earlobe Lad. His super-sized ears and super-hearing made him the perfect target for someone as obnoxious as Boom Boy.

"Man," Boom Boy said in a sad voice. "I don't even feel like blowing up."

"Maam pah ma pamm mam?" Boy-in-the-Plastic-Bubble Boy asked as he slowly rolled over in his Giant Hamster Ball of Justice.

"I don't want to talk about it," Boom Boy said.

Spelling Beatrice was sitting next to Spice Girl, who was now chatting with Charisma Kid.

Exact Change Kid was making page after page of notes: small scribbles, detailed descriptions, and elaborate theories.

"To follow Rule #1 breaks Rule #2, but to follow Rule #2 breaks Rule #1 . . ." He took his eraser and aggressively rubbed it against the page. "What am I overlooking? *What?*"

"Please don't erase so loud!" Earlobe Lad complained.

I walked up and saw the whole group sitting on the curb. They all looked sad, except for Spice Girl, who was taking advantage of the free time to talk with Charisma Kid.

"Did he kick you out, too?" Spelling Beatrice asked the moment I sat down next to her.

"Yeah," I replied.

"What rule did *you* break?" Boom Boy inquired, curious to see if it was the same rule he had broken.

"Rule #8," I answered.

"Rule #8?!" Exact Change Kid blurted. "There's a Rule #8?!"

"Yeah," I said, and quoted, "'Rule #8: Never be the last sidekick.'"

Chapter Seven
The Lucky Chapter . . . Or IS It?

The next day we were all back at the Sidekick Super Clubhouse. Pumpkin Pete had told King Justice that he had kicked all of us out of the Sidekicks for breaking the rules. King Justice had then reminded Pumpkin Pete that that meant Pete would have to do his own laundry and get his own Chinese takeout and polish the rims on the Pumpkinmobile himself.

Pete reinstated all of us in less than fifteen minutes.

And in fact, to make sure that would never happen again if he ever had to kick all of us out of the Sidekicks again, Pete approved the Side-kicks to interview for a brand new member. That way, there'd be one leftover sidekick to do his chores. Pete suggested we name the new sidekick "Chore Boy" or "Task Lass."

Exact Change Kid, Boom Boy, and Boy-in-the-Plastic-Bubble Boy sat behind the Sidekick Super Fold-Out Table, or in Boy-in-the-Plastic-Bubble Boy's case, sat in his Giant Hamster Ball of Justice behind the Sidekick Super Fold-Out Table in the middle of the Sidekick Super Additional-Parking Parking Lot of Justice. The rest of us flanked them on either side, except for Charisma Kid, who had told us to "pick whatever stupid new sidekick you want" and to try not to choose "as big a loser as the rest of you."

Several would-be sidekicks lined up on the opposite side of the table. Exact Change Kid pulled out a clipboard and read the first name.

"Super Vision Lad?"

A young boy stepped forward. He had a wild look in his eyes, and his head darted about. He had black hair and a beach towel clothespinned around his neck, like a terry cloth cape. Otherwise, he was dressed totally normal, in jeans and a T-shirt that said MOMMY'S LITTLE ANGEL. One of his shoes was untied and he had a runny nose. His mother was with him and held him firmly by the wrist.

"So . . . you have super eyes, I see," Exact Change Kid said. "How far can you see?"

"He doesn't have super eyes," Super Vision Lad's mother corrected.

Super Vision Lad made motorboat noises with his lips, extended his arms, and spun around like a human helicopter. "I like chocwet!" he yelled.

"Then why is he called Super Vision Lad?" Boom Boy asked.

"Because he needs constant supervision," the kid's mother answered.

"How does that power work?" Spice Girl asked.

"Look, I'll pay you ten dollars an hour if he can joined your little 'club' from three to six every day." His mother pulled out thirty dollars and laid it on the table. "And double on holidays. I just . . . I just need a little break."

Exact Change Kid looked at the other side-kicks. "Well, we might have to fight evil during those hours . . ."

"Does it take *all* of you to fight evil?" Super Vision Lad's mother asked.

"Usually," Spelling Beatrice jumped in. "Don't you think you'd be better off finding a babysitter?"

"Oh, I see how it is," Super Vision Lad's

mother said in a huff. "You can count pennies and spell words and roll around in a plastic hamster ball and suddenly you're too good for ten dollars an hour?"

"MAAA PA MAA PAM!" Boy-in-the-Plastic-Bubble Boy yelled.

I turned and saw Super Vision Lad kicking Boy-in-the-Plastic-Bubble Boy's Giant Hamster Ball of Justice around the Sidekick Super Additional-Parking Parking Lot of Justice like he was a giant plastic soccer ball with a screaming teenager inside.

"I told you he needed constant supervision!" his mother snarled, and chased after her son.

"Next!" Boom Boy called out.

A boy with a large, brown cardboard box encasing his body stepped forward. There were holes cut out for his head and legs, and the box covered his body from his shoulders down to just below his hips.

"I'm Boy-in-the-Cardboard-Box Boy!" he said eagerly.

"And what powers do you have?" Exact Change Kid asked.

"Cardboard powers!" Boy-in-the-Cardboard-Box Boy bragged.

"Wow," Spice Girl whispered to Spelling Beatrice. "He *is* powerful."

"Powerful?" I quietly butted in. "What makes *him* so powerful?"

"He can stack himself," Spice Girl explained. "And I can store my winter clothes in him."

"That doesn't make him powerful," I huffed.

Spice Girl turned her back to me. "Let's see if you're still saying that when summer comes."

"Hey, hey!" Boom Boy said. "Here's a little test for you: What would you do if the Veggie Tarian attacked you with his Cucumber Brigade and you were the only one who could stop him?"

Boy-in-the-Cardboard-Box Boy laughed as if the answer was obvious. "I possess all the powers of cardboard! I'd simply defeat him with that!"

Exact Change Kid and Boom Boy looked Boy-in-the-Cardboard-Box Boy over. "I don't know," Boom Boy said, shaking his head. "I just don't think you've got what it takes to be a sidekick. Unless we can store our winter clothes in you when summer comes."

"Sorry, BITCBB," Exact Change Kid said, and checked a box labeled LOSER on his clipboard.

"Oh, I get it now, you can have a kid in a Giant Hamster Ball, but not one in a Giant

Cardboard Box?!" Boy-in-the-Cardboard-Box Boy shouted.

"MAAAA PA MAM PAM!" Boy-in-the-Plastic-Bubble Boy yelled in a panic as Super Vision Lad rolled him across the street and into the deserted field.

"Come back here with that hamster ball!" Super Vision Lad's mother yelled, and chased after him.

"It's nothing against you," Exact Change Kid explained. "Boy-in-the-Plastic-Bubble Boy's got a Giant Hamster Ball of Justice . . ."

"And you're just stuck in a stupid brown box!" Boom Boy cut in. "You look like a rectangle turd!"

"Don't make me smite you with my Giant Cardboard Box of Justice!" Boy-in-the-Cardboard-Box Boy threatened.

"Oh yeah? Oh yeah?" Boom Boy stood up. "You just try and I'll blow up so good, there won't be enough of your box left to line a birdcage!"

"I'd like to see you try!" Boy-in-the-Cardboard-Box Boy dared.

And with that, Boom Boy jumped to the other side of the table and balled his fists. He clenched his teeth so tightly that deep lines formed in his cheeks.

"Cardboard Powers, activate!" Boy-in-the-

Cardboard-Box Boy shouted. He charged Boom Boy and repeatedly bashed into him with his cardboard box. "Take that! And that! And that!" he yelled with each collision.

"Let's see . . . how good are you . . . with that box . . . when I blow you . . . to the . . . moon!" Boom Boy threatened between gritted teeth.

"Super Box Attack!" Boy-in-the-Cardboard-Box Boy yelled. He spun in place and bashed Boom Boy with the sides of his cardboard box.

"Oh no! Boom Boy's losing!" Spice Girl gasped.

Earlobe Lad peeked his head out from under the table. Both of his hands were clasped over his ears. "Well I sure wish he'd lose a little more quietly," he whispered up to us.

"How can you tell he's losing?" I asked.

"Because he looks so sad," she replied.

"Maybe we should move the table back," Exact Change Kid said. "If Boom Boy really blows up, I don't want to get his parts all over my costume. My mom just washed it."

Boom Boy bent over and crossed his arms over his stomach. He grunted twice and his face grew a shade of deep red.

"He's not going to blow up," I said.

"How do you know?" Exact Change Kid was already moving his chair back.

"Because he *never* blows up," I reminded him.

Suddenly Boom Boy unclenched his fists and stood up. "Wait! I get it now. I get it. You *want* me to blow up, don't you?" Boom Boy said to me. "Yeah. 'Cause once I do, I'll be gone and —"

"Take that! And that! And that!" Boy-in-the-Cardboard-Box Boy yelled. He charged Boom Boy and repeatedly bashed into him with his Cardboard Box of Justice.

"Could you hold on just a second?" Boom Boy said to him, and then turned to me. "Now where was I?"

"Wait! I get it now. I get it. You *want* me to blow up, don't you?" I mimicked Boom Boy, which was easy enough to do since I've heard his speech so many times.

"Oh yeah! That's right! 'Cause once I do, I'll be gone and then there'll be no more Boom Boy and you won't be able to say that he *never* blows up!"

"But Boom Boy, you never *do* blow up! You just threaten to," I reminded him.

"And that's how it better stay, or I swear, I swear . . . I'll blow myself up!"

"Okay, okay! How about Boxy: The Box Boy?" Boy-in-the-Cardboard-Box Boy asked hopefully. "Can I be a sidekick then?"

"Are you still here?" Boom Boy asked.

"Why don't you just leave your name and number and if we ever have a future vacancy, we'll give you a call," Spelling Beatrice suggested, a lone voice of reason.

That's one thing I really, really like about Spelling Beatrice. Not only does she not drive me absolutely insane like the other sidekicks do, but she acts like she actually has a brain in her head. I used to think it was because she was the oldest, but then I realized she seems totally sane because the other sidekicks are just totally insane.

Boy-in-the-Cardboard-Box Boy wrote his name and phone number on a piece of paper and handed it to Exact Change Kid. Then he slumped in his box like a sad little piece of cardboard who had just found out he was really only a piece of notebook paper.

I mean, I don't know if cardboard would be sad if it ever found out it was just a piece of notebook paper, but I'm guessing it would.

Boom Boy looked over Exact Change Kid's shoulder and eyed the piece of paper. "He just broke Rule #1," Boom Boy giggled.

"Next!" Exact Change Kid called out.

A kid in a hamster costume stepped up, holding his father's hand. The cheap, oversized costume head was held on by Velcro. "I'm Hamster

Man!" the kid immediately said with a huge smile.

"Sorry!" Boom Boy said quickly. "Boys, Kids, Girls, Lasses, Gals, Lads, and Juniors only. No Mans or Womans allowed. NEXT!"

Hamster Man pulled his hand away from his father. "I told you it should be Hamster Boy! I told you! I told you! I told you!" He lifted his furry paws to his eyes and ran across the League of Big Justice Super Additional-Parking Parking Lot of Justice. "I don't wanna go back to the pet store!" he yelled.

"Maybe this was a bad idea," Spelling Beatrice said to me.

"When is anything that we do *not* a bad idea?" I answered.

"I should be practicing my Grammar Powers now."

Spelling Beatrice's statement brought two very important questions to mind:

QUESTION #1
How do you practice Grammar Powers?

QUESTION #2
What in the world *are* Grammar Powers?

"Well . . . I put on a blindfold and write noun-modifying sentences with subordinate clauses without dangling my participles or splitting any infinitives," Spelling Beatrice informed me.

Did I say she was sane?

"And then what?" I asked.

"I take off the blindfold and see how good I did," she replied.

"Don't you mean how *well* you did?" I asked.

Spelling Beatrice went white, like she was choking on an onomatopoeia. Her left eye twitched. She grabbed my elbow and pulled me closer.

"This stays between you and me!" she begged.

Chapter Nine
Princess Floppo the Fish Girl

Boom Boy held his palm up to his mouth and checked his breath. Satisfied it wasn't too offensive, he started the difficult line of questioning. "So, what planet do you come from, Princess Floppo?" He sounded excited that he was meeting a real princess from another planet.

"Earth." Princess Floppo said.

"Wow. Her planet has the same name as ours!" Spice Girl gushed and clapped her hands together. "Hurray for Earth!"

"I think she *is* from the same planet as us," I said to Spice Girl.

"I'm not from her planet, silly! I'm from this one," Spice Girl said, and shook her head in disbelief.

"And she's from this planet, too," I explained.

"No, she's not, Mr. Know-It-All." Spice Girl rolled her eyes. "She said she's from 'Earth.'" Spice Girl punctuated her remark with finger quotes.

I don't even know why I bother.

"MAAA PAM MAM MAM PAH MAAAAA!" Boy-in-the-Plastic-Bubble Boy shouted in terror as Super Vision Lad pushed his Giant Hamster Ball of Justice down a hill in the vacant field across the street.

"So are you a princess of some country?" Exact Change Kid asked. Luckily, he understood what Princess Floppo meant when she said complicated things like "I'm from Earth."

"No," Princess Floppo replied.

"An island?"

"Nope."

"An independent conglomeration of city-states?"

"A what?"

"What *are* you princess of?" I asked.

"Nothing really, I guess. I just always wanted

to be a princess," Princess Floppo replied. "And I like ponies."

Exact Change Kid looked at his clipboard. "I see here that your full name is Princess Floppo the Fish Girl. Can you breathe underwater? Swim super fast? Ride dolphins?"

"I'm afraid of the water," Princess Floppo stated.

"Do you have fish powers?" Boom Boy asked, hopefully.

"Or *any* powers?" I added.

"Of course! I have the power to flop around like a fish out of water." And with that, Princess Floppo fell to the ground and flopped about like a . . . like a . . . well . . . like a giant fish out of water. She flipped and flopped and flopped and flipped.

Boom Boy watched for a moment, then leaned back in his chair. "She gets my vote."

"What? How is she going to fight evil by flopping around on the ground like a fish?" I snapped.

"Hey, when you joined the Sidekicks, no one asked how you were going to fight evil by running around!" Boom Boy reminded me.

"But I can run 108 miles per hour!"

"And your point is what, exactly?" Boom Boy replied.

"I have a *super power*! I don't just flop around on the ground like a fish!"

"If you think it's so easy, let's see you try!" Boom Boy huffed back.

"You're missing my point," I sighed.

"I'm not," Spice Girl jumped in. "Your point is that there *aren't* two planets named Earth and that Princess Floppo is only saying the name of the planet where she's princess is 'Earth' because she doesn't want to tell us the real name of her home planet and break Rule #1."

"Rule #1?" I inquired.

"Yes! 'Never tell anyone the name of the planet you live on.' Didn't you listen to anything Peter Pumpkin said?" Spice Girl wondered.

Right now, I was really wondering what planet Spice Girl lived on.

"Rule #1 is 'Never tell anyone your real name,'" I reminded her.

"Nah! That was Rule #9!" Boom Boy joined in.

"There is no Rule #9!" I argued.

"I have a rule for you!" Earlobe Lad whispered from beneath the table. "SHUT UP!"

"Oh! That's a good one," Spice Girl said, and gave Earlobe Lad a quiet thumbs-up. "But I just broke it, didn't I? Oops! I broke it again! Oops! I did it again!"

"Uh, guys," Exact Change Kid cut in. "Maybe we should stop Princess Floppo before continuing with this discussion?"

I looked over to the floor. Princess Floppo still flipped and flopped about like a . . . like a . . . well . . . like a giant fish out of water.

"She certainly is determined," I admitted.

Princess Floppo the Fish Girl stood up and brushed the dirt from her Spandex costume. Although she had none of the powers of a fish, had no gills, no tail, and wasn't even a princess, she still wore a small fake-diamond encrusted tiara. Her outfit had large, glittery imitation green fish scales that looked like she had pulled them off an ugly evening gown. On her back was a green fin made from some wavy material that was probably once a kite.

"My mom helped me stitch it," she confessed as Boom Boy pulled out a chair for her.

Luckily, there was only one more person who had come for the sidekick tryouts. She was younger than most of the other hopefuls, but she wore a ninja outfit. Man! It'd be awesome to have a sidekick who could really kick butt, someone who knew the martial arts and could really punch evil in the face! Roundhouses! Spinning kicks! No-shadow punches! Nunchucks! Throwing stars! Butt-kicking —

"Twick or tweat!" the girl yelled giddily and held out a plastic candy holder shaped like a jack-o-lantern.

"Ahhh! Leave me alone!" Earlobe Lad called out from under the table. Apparently, the sound of my head repeatedly banging the Sidekick table was hurting his giant ears.

Chapter Ten
I Have a Headache!

"I have the worst headache," I said after banging my head several times on the table.

"*You* have a headache?" Earlobe Lad mumbled from under the table. "Welcome to *my* life! And stop blinking so loud!"

That was when my phone rang.

"Spuddy! Spuddy!" Pumpkin Pete's voice cried out over my cell phone. "I need your help!"

"It's not laundry day!" I replied.

"No! Something worse! I — hey! Hey! Get away from me! Don't! No! Aaaah!"

Pete's phone went dead. He really was in trouble! I leaped from my chair. "Gotta run!" I said, and jumped up to head for the League of Big Justice.

"Hey! Speedy! You haven't voted for the new sidekick!" Exact Change Kid said.

"Can't vote now! Gotta save Pete!"

"What's with that guy and never wanting to vote?" Boom Boy asked.

"Maybe he just doesn't like democracy," Exact Change Kid commented.

"It's probably because Spelling Beatrice always beats him when they play it," Spice Girl commented.

"That's *Scrabble*," Spelling Beatrice corrected.

Exact Change Kid pulled out the ballots and handed them to the other sidekicks. He dropped one under the table for Earlobe Lad.

"I need a pencil," he mumbled. "And could you *please* not drop it so loudly? And whose stomach is gurgling? Aaah! Will everyone *please* eat lunch before these meetings? Is that too much to ask?"

I ran through the League of Big Justice Super Justice Lobby and past the League of Big Justice Super Souvenir Gift Shop of Justice, and that was when I saw him. Pumpkin Pete came racing toward me like the building was on fire, or at least like it was Halloween night and an angry pumpkin-carving mob was on the loose.

"Spuddy! Spuddy! You gotta help me! It's terrible! Terrible!" Pete shouted.

"What is it, Pete? Is evil attacking? Is King Justice in trouble? Is it an angry pumpkin-carving mob on the loose?" You never know.

Pete collapsed and I caught his big, fat, orange pumpkin head with both hands. "The horror! The horror!"

"What's happening, Pete?! You have to tell me!"

"He's evil! Pure evil!" Pete's head slumped in my arms. And that was when I saw it.

"Where big orange bawoon man?" Super Vision Lad yelled, racing around the corner toward us.

Pete jumped up and hid behind me. "Get that monster away from me!"

"Pete! It's just Super Vision Lad!" I assured him.

"Super Vision Lad, or the greatest evil the world has ever known?" Pete gasped.

I looked at Super Vision Lad. He made a spit bubble between his lips. It popped, and he giggled, "I wike bubbose!"

"The kid's mother . . . she tricked me! Promised me ten bucks an hour if I watched him until six o'clock! The kid's unstoppable! She should pay me a hundred dollars a minute!"

"Well, Pete, what're you going to do?"

"I'm not going to do anything! It's your problem now!" Pete informed me, and pushed me toward Super Vision Lad.

"Me? I don't want to babysit this kid! I'm a sidekick! I have to be ready to fight evil at all times!" I couldn't believe Pete was trying to pawn this kid off on me.

What am I saying? Of course I could believe it.

"You want to fight evil?" Pete asked. "Just turn your back on that kid for ten seconds. I swear, he needs constant supervision!"

"Tacos are funny!" Super Vision Lad shouted, and started banging his head against the display stand of Pumpkin Pete action figures at the League of Big Justice Super Souvenir Gift Shop. One of the action figures fell off the top shelf.

"I have all the powers of a pumpkin!" the action figure boasted when it hit the floor. Super Vision Lad picked up the doll and began to chew on its big, fat, orange pumpkin head.

"You break it, you buy it!" Pete shouted, and then immediately ducked behind me again.

"Look, Pete, I have to get back to the other sidekicks and vote," I informed him. "By this time, they probably think I really, really hate democracy."

"And well you should!" Pete snorted. "I hear that Spelling Beatrice always kicks your butt when you play."

I didn't have a clue what he was talking about. But then, I almost never had a clue about what

Pete was talking about. Or Exact Change Kid. Or Spice Girl, Boom Boy, Earlobe Lad, and Boy-in-the-Plastic-Bubble Boy.

Oddly enough, though, I knew exactly what Boy-in-the-Cardboard-Box Boy had been talking about.

"Sorry, Pete. I have to go," I told him, and started to head down the hall. "I have to play in my first football game tonight."

It's a long story, but basically, I lost my temper one day at school when Mandrake Steel (a.k.a. Charisma Kid) was taunting me in front of Prudence Cane (a.k.a. The Girl I Have a Crush On But Doesn't Even Know I'm Alive Even Though I Sit Next to Her in Class). So I used just a little bit of my super speed to make Mandrake look stupid, and the school's football coach saw me. Let's just say he made me the starting running back on the spot.

Sure, I'm too small to play. Sure, I'd never played real football before the first team practice, and sure, I was more scared to play in tonight's game than when I saw Pumpkin Pete blasting off from Pluto in the final escape rocket, but I figure a little super speed goes a long way.

Or at least it goes far enough to help me avoid

any broken bones when the padded giants on the other team try to squish me.

I was almost safely out the door when Pete shouted, "Wait! You can't go! Don't you remember Rule #2?"

I froze. Nailed on a technicality!

I turned around, and in a deeply sighing breath said, "'Rule #2: No matter how crazy it sounds, no matter how dangerous you think it may be, always, always do what a superhero asks you to do.'"

"Nah!" Pete scolded. "That's Rule #9!"

"There is no Rule #9!"

"If there's no Rule #9, then how come you just recited it to me, smart guy?"

"Because that was Rule #2!" I said.

"Weren't you paying any attention when I trained you yesterday?" Pete slapped his forehead with his viney hand. "Rule #2 is — and *please* try to pay attention this time — Rule #2 is: You have to baby-sit. See ya!"

Pete turned and raced down the League of Big Justice Super Justice Lobby. "Pumpkin feets, don't fail me now!" he yelped.

"Do I at least get to keep the ten dollars?" I shouted.

Pete skidded to a stop at the door to the

League of Big Justice Inner Sanctum of Justice. "Are you kidding? All money earned by a superhero goes to charity!" he called back.

I thought for a moment, then shook my head. "And let me guess, you're donating this money to the Charity to Help Persons with Big, Fat, Orange Pumpkin Heads?"

"Bingo!" Pete said and slammed the door behind him.

The thing is, Pumpkin Pete *is* the only person with a big, fat, orange head.

Like a pumpkin.

Chapter Twelve
2 + 2 = EVIL!

I looked at Super Vision Lad as he chewed the head off the Pumpkin Pete doll and spit it onto the floor. The head bounced across the gray marble and rolled to a stop at the edge of the Hall of Heroes of Big Justice.

"Since I'm stuck babysitting you for a few hours, you might as well tell me your real name," I said.

"Soap tastes bad!" Super Vision Lad shouted.

"Fine. I'll just call you Super Vision Lad. How'd you like to go play in the park across the street?"

"Soap tastes bad!" Super Vision Lad shouted, and head-butted me in the stomach.

We walked across the street to the park. Well,

it used to be a park. About a month ago, Sunburneo attacked the League of Big Justice with his solar satellite. His calculations were off a bit (he forgot to carry the "2") and instead of melting the League of Big Justice, he just burned the park across the street to a crisp. Now it was just a vacant field with a melted slag heap that used to be monkey bars.

Super Vision Lad and I sat on the blackened grass and suddenly, a very strange thing happened. No, Super Vision Lad didn't stop kicking me in the shin. Nor did he stop yelling "The itsy-bitsy spidah! The itsy-bitsy spidah!" No, what happened was, the melted slag heap that was once monkey bars slowly dissolved into nothingness. Then, the charcoaled remains of a nearby tree dissolved as well.

"Uh . . . maybe we should get the heck out of here," I said to Super Vision Lad, but it was too late. Evil was upon us.

"Well, helllllooo, my little goggled one! Are you the champion of the League of Big Justice come to do battle? I didn't expect him to be so . . . goggled. But no bother! You shall fall before the decaying might of The Candy Man!"

"The Candy Man? Am I supposed to be afraid or hope you'll give me a chocolate bar?"

"Oh, llllaugh while you can, chimpanzee of goodness. But once I attack with my rainbow of fruit flavors, we shall see who is llllaughing!"

"Probably still me."

I looked at The Candy Man. He was tall and very thin. He had narrow shoulders and long, narrow arms. His long, thin legs were like short stilts. He wore a pinkish waistcoat with a frilly shirt. On his head was a tooth. A very large, oversized tooth that strapped under his chin like an enormous water bucket on his head. In his right hand, he held a cane. Actually, he held a large *candy*-cane cane.

"I mean, what're you going to do? Pelt me with Skittles or something?" I asked. I pressed my palm against Super Vision Lad's forehead and gently pushed him back so he'd stop head-butting me.

"Oh! I shhhhall do far worse than that! I shall ssspread candy and chocolate throughout the world for all to eat! Bwahahahaha!" The Candy Man thrust both fists in the air as if he had just won a championship boxing match.

I took Super Vision Lad by the hand and started to walk away. "Go ahead," I said.

"How dare you turn your back on The Candy Man!"

"What? You're going to give free candy and chocolate to people. You want me to fight you over *that*?"

"But their teeth . . . they'lllll . . . rot out! Yes! Rot right out! And the dentists! The dentists will make lotsss of money, and no one likes dentists! Bwahahahaha!"

"Nice try."

"Then the chocolate will melt and . . . they will get it on their clothes and have to wash them . . . and . . . then all the extra detergent will wash to the sssea and poison the waters! Bwahahahaha —" He stopped laughing and gave me an eager look.

"I doubt it."

"But the sssugar! All the sssugar will make everyone very hyper and —"

"You didn't really think this out very well before you came, did you?" I cut in.

"Welllll. No . . . perhaps I did get a little excited when I got my new candy shhhipment this morning," The Candy Man confessed. "But the costume! The costume I have been working on for months!" He proudly rapped the large tooth attached to his head.

"Look, I'm not one to go around giving super

villains advice, but you really need . . . like . . . a theme. And a plan. Something that'll really get people's attention and make them wonder if you really will be the next ruler of the earth."

"But I don't want to rule the earth! I just want to give everyone cavities! And then rule the earth! Must do thingsss in the proper order, my Jujube of Justice!"

The Candy Man thrust out both of his arms and revealed two small chocolate rockets. They targeted me and shot from his wrists. I grabbed Super Vision Lad and rolled out of the way just in time. The twin chocolate rockets hit a burnt tree and melted it on impact.

"Rot it away, my sssweet, sssweet treats!" The Candy Man shouted. "Rot the chewy goodness that stands between us and worldwide cavities!"

This guy may have a stupid name and an even stupider costume, but there's one thing I've learned since becoming a sidekick: No matter how dumb the villain, he can probably do a real good job of blowing things up.

Or in this case, rotting them away like a cavity rots teeth.

The League of Big Justice could deal with The

Candy Man easily enough, but I had to protect Super Vision Lad. I snatched him off the ground and raced back across the street to the League of Big Justice.

"Twains go 'choo-choo'!" Super Vision Lad shouted, and bit my ear.

Chapter Thirteen
The Candy Man Can

"Pete! Pete! You've got to help me!" I shouted into the video screen. Pete had retreated to the Inner Sanctum of Big Justice — the place where only members of the League of Big Justice could go — and locked the vault-sized door behind him. I held Super Vision Lad firmly by the waist and hit the intercom button again. "Pete!"

I felt a strong shuddering behind me and saw The Candy Man dissolve the King Justice display in the League of Big Justice Super Souvenir Gift Shop of Justice. "Say hellllo to the Milk Dud of Mayhem!"

"PETE!"

The screen finally flickered on. "What? Who's there?"

"Pete! It's me! Speedy! I need your help!"

"I bet you do! That kid's a monster!"

"No, Pete! The League of Big Justice is under attack!" I shouted into the intercom. "If you could just let in Super Vision Lad while I —"

"Oh no!" Pete shouted into the intercom. "I'm not falling for *that* one! You're on your own!"

"Pete! I swear we're under attack!"

"We are *not* under attack. If we were, I would be beating up the villain right now! And, since I am not beating up any villain but am sitting in my Super Pumpkin Slippers and enjoying a nice bowl of ice cream, then we in fact cannot be under attack!" He paused and shoveled a large scoop of ice cream into his mouth and thought for a moment. "Because if we were under attack, as I have already pointed out, I would be beating up the villain right now! And, since I am not beating up any —"

"I get the point, Pete."

I turned from the video screen and watched The Candy Man throw a fistful of colorful chocolate Easter eggs at the statue of King Justice. Its head dissolved like sugar in hot water. "Beware the Junior Mint of Madnesss!"

The Candy Man stopped for a moment and leaned on his candy-cane cane. Then he started to sing. "Oh! Who can take a sssidekick, melt him into goo? Cover him in chocolate and King Justice, too? The Candy Man! The Candy Man can!" He spun around on his candy-cane cane and clicked his heels in the air. "Oh, The Candy Man can, 'cause he made deadly candy and his own costume, too!" He did a quick tap dance move, spun around, and blasted the display of League of Big Justice action figures with his candy cane. Then, as suddenly as he had started his little musical number, he stopped. "Oh, sssidekick! I've got sssome candy that'll melt in your mouth and in your hands — literally!"

I spun back around to the video monitor. "Come on, Pete! Just this once!"

"Sorry! Pete's babysitting service closed one hour ago!" The monitor went black.

The Candy Man laughed and lifted his candy cane. "Here comes the Milky Way of Malice!" He blasted the statues of Ms. Mime, Captain Haggis, and Mr. Ironic. Actually, The Candy Man had aimed for The Good Egg. But as he fired, he stumbled over an action figure of Mr. Ironic from the League of Big Justice Super Souvenir Gift Shop of Justice, and his blast glanced to the left, accidentally blowing up Mr. Ironic's statue.

He'd run out of things to destroy pretty soon. I had to get Super Vision Lad to safety. I kneeled before Super Vision Lad and gently held him by the shoulders.

"I need you to be strong for me, little guy," I said in a calm voice. "I need you to run out of that giant hole in the wall and go hide. Don't be afraid. I'll make sure The Candy Man doesn't hurt you, okay? But I can't fight him and protect you at the same time. Are you ready to be brave?"

Super Vision Lad looked at me for a moment. Then he kicked my shin and shouted, "Mud tastes icky!"

And to think . . . for this I gave up being a junior assistant florist.

"My, my, my!" The Candy Man closed in on me. "What do you think of my plan, you little Reese's Peanut Butter Punk? Have I gotten the 'theme' right? Dissolve. Destroy. Spread cavities. Rule the world. Sounds good to me!"

I picked up Super Vision Lad and flopped him over my shoulder like a potato sack. The hole in the wall wasn't too far away, but running indoors and carrying Super Vision Lad would make this more difficult than getting my mom to raise my allowance.

Actually, nothing was more difficult than getting my mom to raise my allowance.

I ran to the left. The Candy Man flung several licorice sticks. They flopped about on the ground, discharging enough electricity to stop an elephant . . . and unfortunately, I was no elephant. I picked up my speed and jumped over the electrical hazard — and right into the awaiting gumdrop attack of The Candy Man.

Green! Yellow! Orange! Red! And some brownish-purple color I think they call indigo! The gumdrops stuck to my outfit and started to dissolve the Spandex.

"They're chewy *and* deadly!" The Candy Man shouted. "Am I brilliant, or what?"

I could feel the gumdrops starting to burn my skin. But I couldn't give up. Sure, I had to save Super Vision Lad and bring The Candy Man's sugary reign of terror to an end, but there was something more. I had to prove to myself that my dad was wrong, that I shouldn't just be junior assistant florist. I made a choice. I took the League of Big Justice oath, and *this* was the reason why.

No, not to be pelted with candy by some kook with a giant tooth on his head, but because I wanted to be a hero. Sure, some heroes deliver flowers, some heroes babysit kids, and some heroes flip burgers over a flame grill, but I wanted to be a hero who would rise up as a force for good and halt the chocolate-covered madness that tried to bend the world to its sugar-frosted ways.

What the heck was I talking about? I don't know. Maybe the pain made me delirious. Maybe it was The Candy Man's terrible singing, or his abuse of my favorite candies, or maybe it was just the tasty little gumdrops that were painfully burning brightly colored circles into my skin, but at that moment, more than ever before, I just wanted to punch evil in the face!

I tightened my grip on Super Vision Lad, raced toward The Candy Man at 87 miles per hour, leaped into the air, and delivered a surprise kick right to his jaw.

The Candy Man fell to one knee. Dozens of M&Ms fell from his waistcoat and bounced on the ground.

"Candyyy!" Super Vision Lad called out and tried to squirm free.

The Candy Man felt his jaw. "Well ssstruck,

sssidekick. But boy, am I gonna kick the cream filling out of you!"

I didn't wait around to see what he had in mind. I raced out of the gaping hole in the side of the League of Big Justice and toward the Side-kick Super Clubhouse.

"Hey! Come back!" The Candy Man yelled after me. "I can't run that fast with all this caramel in my pockets!"

Chapter Fourteen

"Where is everybody?!" I shouted. No answer. The Sidekick Super Clubhouse was empty. I didn't have much time before The Candy Man found me. I called out again.

Nothing.

That was when I saw it. No, not the key to defeating The Candy Man. Not the sugar-coated remains of the Sidekicks. Heck, it wasn't even a babysitter's phone number. It was a note.

Dear Speedy,

We went to Burger Barn with the League of Big Justice to celebrate the addition of our

*new sidekick. Come join us if you'd like!
King Justice is buying.*

*Sincerely,
Exact Change Kid
Sidekick*

*P.S. Pumpkin Pete is on monitor duty. Call
him if you need anything or an emergency
happens.*

I crumpled the note and threw it to the ground. I don't know what ticked me off more: having to fight evil all by myself (again), or that King Justice was buying dinner for everyone and I was stuck fighting some candy-throwing goofball with a giant tooth on his head!

Super Vision Lad pulled one of the burning gumdrops from my skin and stuck it in his mouth.

"No!" I shouted.

"Tastes like owwie!" Super Vision Lad yelped, and spit the blue gumdrop to the ground.

I had a few moments before The Candy Man found me with his Candy Corn of Doom or Chocolate Kisses of Severe Pain or something. I knocked all the burning gumdrops from my skin. Then I remembered.

I ran to the far side of the Sidekick Super Clubhouse Room of Meetingness and quickly pounded on a door that stood in the middle of the wall.

"Whaddaya want?" A voice yelled from the room on the other side.

"I need your help! Can I come in?" I called back.

"Aw, man! Whatever."

I opened the door and there was Latchkey Kid sitting on the couch, watching TV.

"Hey, how're you doing?" I asked.

"Nothing," he said without looking up.

"No, I said *how*'re you doing, not *what*'re you doing."

"Whatever."

"So . . . uh . . . I'm really sorry to bug you, but would you mind watching Super Vision Lad for me?" I gently moved Super Vision Lad in front of me.

"Aw, man!" Latchkey Kid groaned. "Do I have to?"

"No, but it would really help me out a lot. It's a beautiful day outside. Maybe you two could go to the park or something."

"The park's burnt and filled with charcoal!" Latchkey Kid complained.

"I could give you a few dollars for ice cream . . ."

"I wanted to watch the Jackie Chan movie marathon on TV!" Latchkey Kid griped.

"You still can! And you guys can order pizza. You like pizza, don't you?" I asked hopefully.

"Pizzaaaaa!" Super Vision Lad yelled. "Yaaaay!"

"I guess so," Latchkey Kid admitted.

"Great. Just keep Super Vision Lad safe," I reminded him. "And maybe when I get back, we can all go to the movies or something."

"Whatever." Latchkey Kid stared at the TV and took a big swig of his Pow! Soda.

I nudged Super Vision Lad into the room and made sure they locked the door behind me.

"You know, sssometimes you feel like a nut," The Candy Man said from behind me. "Sssometimes you don't." I didn't turn around. I dove away from Latchkey Kid's door as blobs of gooey nougat splattered where I had been standing.

"I'm ready for you now!" I shouted.

"Let's sssee if you're so cocky after you taste a rainbow of fruit flavors!" The Candy Man used his candy-cane cane and blasted a bright, tasty-looking rainbow of energy at me. I ran as fast as I could and narrowly escaped the explosion from the blast.

What I did not avoid was the wad of gum The Candy Man threw at me. "Double your pleasure! Double your fun!" he laughed.

"This isn't fun!" I shouted back. The gum hit the ground in front of me and grew like shaving cream. I tried to zip to the left, but I was running too fast to make a sharp turn. The moment I hit the gum, both my feet stuck like they were stuck in gum. Which made perfect sense, since I *was* stuck in gum.

"Now, before I destroy you and then un-leashhh my awesome cavity powers on the world, making them rue the day they ever invented sssugar-free treats, I do have *one* sssmall question for you."

I knew it. He'd want to know where the League of Big Justice hid the controls for the League of Big Justice Satellite of Super Orbitness, or what the code was to the Inner Sanctum of Justice, or maybe he even wanted to know if I knew King Justice's real name.

Obviously, The Candy Man knew nothing about Rule #1.

"Go ahead! Ask what you want! I won't tell you anything!"

"Awfully brave for a boy I am about to melt."

"I'm not just a boy . . . I'm a *sidekick*!"

"Oh. Good for you. Then it's awfully brave for a *sidekick* I am about to melt."

"Ask anything you want! My secrets will melt with me!" I challenged.

"Tell me thisss and perhaps I shhhall set you free . . ." He paused, as if working up the courage to ask the question. "How many licksss does it take to get to the tootsie roll center of a Tootsie Pop?!" The Candy Man yelled.

"What!? How the heck should I know?" I spat back. My feet weren't going anywhere, which is a really bad thing if your super power is super speed.

"Don't play dumb with me!" The Candy Man growled. "Tell me! Tell me now! I know you know!"

"Dude, I really think all that sugar has totally eaten your brain."

"No! No, it has not! All the other kids knew how many licksss it took to get to the center! But did they tell me? No! They just pointed and laughed at me! 'Clarence doesn't know how many licksss it takes to get to the center! Clarence doesn't know! Clarence doesn't know! Nyah! Nyah! Nyah-nyah! Nyah!'" The Candy Man stuck out his tongue as he relived an old memory. "Well, the last lllaugh ssshall be mine! I'll give them all cavities! I'll melt them all!"

"But that was when you were a kid! You must be thirty years old now!" I was trying to delay him long enough to squirm out from the gum trap. I had freed enough of my foot that I was able to vibrate it at super speed. I could only hope it was enough to break myself free.

"Oh! Ssso what if it was twenty-four years, six months, fourteen days and . . ." — he looked at the candy watch on his wrist — ". . . five hours ago! Ssso what!" The Candy Man shouted back at me. "Ssso what if we're all grown up and my therapist sssays I should be over it! I'll bet *he* always knew how many licksss it took! I'll bet you! I'll bet the kids never pointed at him and said 'the therapist doesn't know how many licksss it takes to get to the center! The therapist doesn't know! The therapist doesn't know! Nyah! Nyah! Nyah-nyah! Nyah!'"

I'd seen a lot of things in my short life. I'd seen Pluto. I'd seen talking puppets. I'd seen other dimensions, and people with pumpkins for heads, and giant robots, and monster worms, and all kinds of nutty stuff. But I'd never seen a grown man jump up and down with fistfuls of gum and candy, and pout like a little boy who had his favorite toy taken away.

Just when you think you've seen it all, you

have to fight a nut with a rainbow of fruit flavors wearing a giant tooth on his head.

The Candy Man moved closer to me. "Perhaps I'll just cover you in caramel and candy sprinkles and let you slowly dissolve." He reached into his pocket and pulled out a handful of colorful birthday cake sprinkles.

This was my last chance. I had to break free or I'd be turned into one big, gross caramel blob. The Candy Man prepared to attack with his kaleidoscope of doom. I had to try something I'd never done before.

I vibrated my whole lower body as fast as I could. The gum began to stretch. I had to ignore the pain shooting up through both my legs. I had to ignore the crazy super villain that was about to cover me in caramel. I had to focus. I had to focus on escaping and then bringing an end to the sweetest threat the world has ever known. I mustered every last ounce of my powers. A loud, high-pitched vibration filled the air and rattled the windows. Not the windows in the Sidekick Super Clubhouse, because we didn't have any. The windows down the street and stuff.

Chapter Fifteen
Earlobe Lad Doesn't Want His French Fries

Earlobe Lad fell on the floor at the Burger Barn and desperately covered both his giant ears with his hands. He rolled under the table and curled into a ball as a high-pitched vibration sound filled the air and rattled the windows.

"Hey! Hey! Can I have your fries?" Boom Boy looked under the table and asked.

Earlobe Lad rocked back and forth. "Gugh!" he grunted, unable to overcome the incredibly loud noise that only he could hear.

Boom Boy shrugged his shoulders and grabbed the remaining fries that sat on the table. "I'll take that as a 'yes.'"

Chapter Sixteen
Sugar Doesn't Hurt People, PEOPLE Hurt People

A thick stream of caramel plopped onto the gum where I had been stuck. Unfortunately for The Candy Man, I was no longer there. My legs felt like they were going to fall off, but I had loosened enough of the gum that I was able to use my super speed and kick my way out like a fish-crazy dolphin chasing a juicy anchovy. Some of the gum still stuck to the bottom of my boots and the backs of my legs, slowing me down and making it hard to turn.

"Would you ssstop running around ssso I can dissolve you!?" The Candy Man yelled. "Really! What kid *doesn't* love dessert?"

"Your candy-coated reign of terror is over,

Candy Man! The only rainbow of flavors you'll be tasting is liberty, justice, and honor!"

"That's not a rainbow!"

"It is, but it's just not very colorful to evil!"

Without Super Vision Lad to worry about, I could use my super speed and hopefully make quick work of The Candy Man — unless he dissolved me first or the gum still stuck to my body interfered.

"And how, exactly, do you intend to stop me? Do you have a giant toothbrush I don't know about? Or perhaps one of your powers is unlimited dental floss?" The Candy Man laughed.

That was it! I had to use his power against him! What's the enemy of all candy? Children! If I could just get five hundred children to gnaw and . . . no . . . that wouldn't work. Maybe ten dentists? No way! They're even more evil than The Candy Man. If I brought ten of *them* together, who knows what chaos would be unleashed! I wasn't willing to take on *that* horrible responsibility.

That was when I got an idea. It wasn't just an idea, but easily the stupidest idea I had ever had — and that included the time I took Earlobe Lad to see the fireworks show.

Boy, that was a spectacle I'll never forget. And I'm not talking about the fireworks.

I raced as fast as I could, zigging and zagging through The Candy Man's cotton candy assault. That was when he whipped out the heavy artillery: S'MORES!

"When you sssat around the campfire as a child saying 'Mommy! Mommy! Can we make more s'mores, please?' I'll bet you never dreamed of the day that s'mores would be your greatest enemy! Super S'mores Smother Attack!" The Candy Man cackled.

I have no idea what a Super S'mores Smother Attack is. And now that I think about it, I don't even know what a *Regular* S'mores Smother Attack is, either.

In one hand, The Candy Man held peanut butter s'mores. In the other hand, the traditional chocolate s'mores treat loved by millions of Boy Scouts across the globe. I had to act fast. In mere moments I was about to face the most awesome onslaught of s'mores the world has ever known. I raced around The Candy Man at 41 miles per hour. Before he could turn to launch his chocolatey attack, I used my super speed and leaped into the air. He spun, but it was too late! At the last second, I rotated so my gum-covered legs and butt were facing him. I hit him in his giant tooth hat — and stuck.

The Candy Man staggered to the left. Then to the right. His legs wobbled. He had suddenly gained more than a hundred pounds directly on top of his head, and he just couldn't carry my extra weight. He grunted, then tried to hit me with his double s'mores attack, but it was too late. The Candy Man toppled face-first to the floor of the Sidekick Super Clubhouse and fell atop the s'mores he held in each hand.

The s'mores he had meant for me.

"You put your chocolate in my peanut butter," The Candy Man moaned, and then collapsed to the floor, unconscious.

I lay on my back, facing the ceiling, as if I were sitting in a chair, my butt firmly stuck with gum to the crown of The Candy Man's tooth hat. My back was stuck to the floor as well, ensuring that even if The Candy Man awoke before the other sidekicks came back, he wasn't going anywhere.

I tried to turn my head to face the door to Latchkey Kid's room. "Uh . . . a little help here!" I called out.

I had been adhered to the ground for about an hour before The Candy Man woke up. He was unable to move because he was stuck to the floor face-first. He shouted evil things that were luckily muffled by the ground. Both his arms were still pinned beneath him, so he couldn't reach the strap to his tooth hat.

That was when Pumpkin Pete finally came into the Sidekick Super Clubhouse looking for Super Vision Lad so he could collect his thirty dollars.

There I was, my butt glued to a giant tooth, lying on my back and facing the ceiling. The Candy Man lay face-down, yelling obscenities into the floor, a splatter of chocolate and peanut butter on either side of him, and his legs kicking like a swimmer.

"I don't even want to know," Pete said and walked right back out the door.

Chapter Eighteen
Why I Hate Charisma Kid
(a.k.a. Mandrake Steel)

"GUY! You're late!" the coach yelled at me. "It's the first game of the season and you can't even show up on time?"

Not only was it the first game of the season, but it was against our biggest rival, the Cleveland Cavs.

"I'm sorry, coach! I would've been here on time, but I had to defeat The Candy Man and save the world from having their teeth rotted away from his cavity plan for world domination!"

Yeah, that's what I *should've* said. What I *did* say was, "Sorry, coach! I forgot!"

Sometimes I really, really hate pledges of

honor. Instead of telling him the truth and being a hero, I had to lie and get chewed out.

Wow. Now that I think about it, I'm probably the only kid in the world who could totally get out of trouble if he tells the truth, but has to tell a lie so he *can* get yelled at. Whose idea was that?

Probably evil's. Or Pumpkin Pete's.

Anyway, I'd been stuck to the ground for about two hours before the Sidekicks returned. Exact Change Kid got a wheelbarrow of mayonnaise and poured it all over us. He said that's what his mother used to do when he got gum in his hair as a kid. I guess it worked okay. I just know it was gross.

I had raced to the game as fast as I could, and I did get there a few minutes before it started. The coach told me to suit up, but he was too angry to let me play. He yelled something about my having to learn responsibility and stuff.

What's more responsible than saving the world from some nougat-throwing nut wearing a giant tooth on his head?

So there I was, dressed in my full football uniform and sitting on the bench like I still had some of The Candy Man's gum stuck on my butt. I scanned the bleachers for my dad. He was near the front. My mom wasn't there. I kind of "forgot" to mention it to her.

The funny thing was, my mom didn't want me to play football. True, she was also worried when I became a sidekick, but when I told her I made the football team, she absolutely refused to sign the parent waiver.

"Those boys are just hooligans!" she had said, and handed back the form, unsigned.

"But Mom! I fight supervillains!" I argued.

"That's different. They're evil," she explained.

"But they're trying to kill me!"

"And don't you think those football players won't be happy if they make you sprain an ankle?" she countered.

How do you argue with *that*? I knew there was no way I could convince her. Once my mom made up her mind, that was that, and nothing, *nothing* could make her change it.

So I just forged her signature.

I should've just told her I was going to be the official benchwarmer, because after tonight, I think that's about all the coach would ever let me be.

And then a very funny thing happened.

No, my dad didn't suddenly burst from the

stands and fly into the sky like a superhero, nor did Prudence Cane stop cheerleading and ask me to the homecoming dance, nor did Mandrake Steel tell the coach that he should put me in the game.

What happened was, Mandrake Steel told the coach he should put me in the game.

Wait, did I say that *did* happen?

The coach had called a time-out, and there was Mandrake, the Charisma Kid, quarterback to the school team, my rival in the Sidekicks and a real pain in my butt outside the Sidekicks, trying to persuade the coach to let me play.

I was so stunned, I looked to the bleachers to see if my dad *was* flying! Heck, I figure if one miracle can happen, why not two? But he just waved to me, spilling his popcorn.

"Look, Coach, we need a touchdown to win, and I know that Guy messed up tonight, but what've we got to lose?" Mandrake asked.

"The game!" the coach shouted back. "It's second down, we've got seventy yards to go, less than two minutes to play, and you want me to put in Guy?! Now?!"

"You've seen how fast he is! He's done great in the practices and you know he would've started if he just got to the game on time. So he's a bone-head! But he's a bonehead who can run fast!"

Something was wrong. Very, very wrong. Charisma Kid had never been nice to me. Well, there was that one time he was nice to me, but that was just so he could trick me and then *not* be nice to me. This was totally weird. There had to be a reason . . . and then it hit me!

Someone found out Mandrake Steel is really Charisma Kid and they're controlling his mind!

Mandrake leaned over to me and whispered, "I know you think someone found out I'm really Charisma Kid and they're controlling my mind, but that's not it."

So much for that theory.

"So what's up, then?" I whispered back.

"I just hate losing," Mandrake answered. "I'll get you that ball. You just do the rest."

The coach looked at Mandrake. "This is our last time-out . . ."

"Don't worry, Coach. I know he can do it," Mandrake assured him. "And I wanted to mention it earlier, but that's a very nice tie you're wearing. I wish *my* dad could pick ties as nice as that."

The coach smiled and looked down at his

necktie. "Really? I wasn't sure when I picked it out —"

"If you coach half as well as you pick ties, we're going to have a championship season," Mandrake said in that thick, syrupy voice he used when he was really pouring it on.

The coach suddenly looked at me. "Get in there, Guy!"

I grabbed my helmet and raced onto the field with Mandrake.

"You're sure no one's controlling your mind?" I asked again, still stunned at what just happened.

Mandrake didn't answer me. He crowded into the huddle and called the play. I squeezed in between two linebackers. I felt like a doll crammed between two elephants. I was probably half the size of the other kids playing football. If it weren't for my super speed, this would've been one painful idea!

"Okay! I-formation, split right, double hook option on three!" Mandrake spat like he was a general. Basically what he said in non-football English was, "I'm giving Guy the ball."

"BREAK!" The team clapped their hands and broke from the huddle.

"You ready, Guy?" Mandrake asked.

"Am I!"

"Good. Good," Mandrake said. The offensive line was getting into position.

I could feel my heart pounding in my chest. The crowd was cheering wildly. Every player on both benches stood in silent anticipation. This was awesome! No. It was more than awesome. It was like something so awesome that you couldn't even say how awesome it was, *that's* how awesome this was. Even though I was a bug compared to all the other players on the field, there was no way they could catch me. All I had to do was use my super speed, zip around the defensive line, race past the defensive safeties, and win the game! The crowd would go wild! I'd be a hero and Prudence Cane would think I was totally cool! It was perfect. No. It was more than perfect. It was *awesome!*

Hurry up and give me the ball, I thought as I bounced around in the backfield.

Mandrake prepared to start the play. "It's just such a shame," I heard him say to himself. I didn't know if he was talking to me or what.

I had to know. "What?" I asked.

"It's just a shame, that's all."

"What's a shame? What are you talking about?" I was getting worried.

Mandrake sadly shook his head and patted me on the back. "I'm saying that it's a shame, you getting kicked out of the Sidekicks."

"WHAT?!"

"Well, you *know* that it's against the League of Big Justice rules to use your powers for personal gain," Mandrake explained innocently. "And I can't think of anything more personal than using them to win a football game. And in front of all these people. King Justice'll totally flip when he finds out."

"He doesn't need to find out!"

"You're right, he doesn't. But you know . . . somehow . . . I think he will." Mandrake gave me a mean wink and a smile. He turned and faced the offensive line. "HIKE!" he shouted. The center snapped the ball into Mandrake's waiting hands. He took three steps back, turned, and slapped the ball into my gut.

I looked up. The bodies of the massive opposing team charged toward me like angry bulls. They grunted, growled, and shouted. They wanted only one thing: to squash me into the ground.

Now I remembered why I hate Charisma Kid (a.k.a. Mandrake Steel).

Chapter Nineteen
Mandrake Steel — 7 Guy Martin — 0

"Gunh!"

If you're wondering what *"Gunh!"* is exactly, I can best describe it as the painful noise you make when four hooligans, each the size of a bus, pummel you into the ground.

I slowly pulled my limbs from the grassy surface and handed the referee the football. I could see the coach jumping up and down and shouting something that I was glad I couldn't hear.

I was also glad I couldn't read lips.

I had tried to avoid getting slaughtered by the other team, but without being able to use my super speed, it was pretty hopeless.

The clock was ticking. We quickly fell into a huddle.

"Same play," Mandrake said.

"What?" one of the linemen shouted. "Are you nuts?"

"I want to run the same play," Mandrake repeated.

"What?" one of the wide receivers shouted. "Are you nuts?"

"I really think Guy can do this," Mandrake insisted.

"What?" I shouted. "Are you nuts?"

But it was too late. The huddle broke and we fell into formation. I watched the opposing team dig into their positions like hungry lions eager to leap on the idiot with the football and pummel him into the ground.

Unfortunately, I would be the idiot with the football.

"Hike!"

Mandrake fell back and slammed the ball into my gut. This time I used a little super speed. Not enough to get kicked out of the League of Big Justice, but just enough that I could maybe not become one with the earth again.

Two defensive tackles broke through the line. I dodged one, zipped around the other, and saw nothing but empty field between me and the end zone! Or maybe it would be better to say that I saw nothing but empty field between me and the end zone until a massive lineman introduced me to the grass. Face-first.

At least this time I gained four yards. So, add that to my loss of seven yards last play and I was only at negative three yards.

The coach was screaming on the sidelines. The clock ticked down to thirty seconds. We had to go seventy-three yards. It was fourth down. Mandrake called a quick huddle.

"Sorry, Guy," he said and patted me on the helmet. "I guess you'll just have to wait until next game to be the hero."

At times like this, I really wish I didn't have any super powers. My life would be so much easier, delivering flowers, not having to hear lame speeches about sacrifice, never getting teleported into the 97th dimension and forced to fight the two-dimensional people of Flatopia. The biggest evil I'd have to face would be a cranky customer who doesn't tip.

But no. I had to wake up one day and run faster than a car. And then I had to wake up the next day and decide I wanted to save the world. And after that, I *still* had to wake up the third day and decide to join the Sidekicks. Man, why didn't I just stay in bed?

Mandrake called a long bomb. He pointed to one of the wide receivers and said, "You're my man." We fell into formation. The center snapped the ball into Mandrake's hands. The wide receiver ran down the sidelines as fast as he could. Mandrake fell back into the passing pocket. He cocked back the football, eyed the wide receiver, and slapped the ball right into my gut.

The coach suddenly did an excellent imitation of Boom Boy, except I thought the coach really would blow up.

I wanted to win the game. I wanted Prudence to notice me. I wanted the crowd to cheer and my dad to be proud. I wanted to be the hero. But most of all, I wanted to wipe the smug look off Mandrake's face.

Yeah. That's what I *wanted* to do. Too bad the apes on the other team also wanted to do something.

See, what they wanted to do, just in case you haven't noticed a trend here, what they wanted to do was to pummel me into the ground.

I'll give you one guess whose wants came true.

They tackled me hard. I made a small squeaking noise as the wind was crushed from my lungs. I felt a pain stab into my arm, felt my knees buckle under the weight, and saw the football pop from my hands and bounce on the ground.

What happened next wasn't very pretty.

Chapter Twenty
What Happened Next That Wasn't Very Pretty

As I disappeared beneath a crushing tackle, Mandrake picked up my fumble and ran seventy-three yards for the game-winning touchdown.

The crowd cheered. The coach jumped with joy. Prudence squealed with delight. The team hoisted Mandrake onto their shoulders and carried him off the field.

He was the hero.

I lay on the ground with a face full of mud. I looked up to the bleachers.

My dad was gone.

Chapter Twenty-One
Next Stop: The Twilight Zone

Buildings and cars blurred by. I raced down darkened alleys and under broken street lamps. I ran from the football field so no one would see me. No one would see me run 108 miles per hour. No one would see my mud- and grass-stained jersey. No one would see the tears.

No one would see me get lifted off the ground and zoom into the sky.

"You!" I shouted the moment he put me down. "What do you want?"

"I saw tonight's game," he replied.

"Good for you. Can you put me back on the ground now?"

The Strike looked around. He had flown us to the top of a bridge support. There was more than enough room for both of us, and we were far away from any prying eyes.

"I've been watching you for some time," The Strike said.

"Uh . . . you *do* realize how creepy that sounds, right?" I looked over the edge. There was no way I could get down without The Strike's help.

On any other night, I would've asked a thousand questions. Why did he save me when I fought Dr. Robot and the Mole Master? Where has he been for the last twelve years? What did he want from me? Why did The Strike leave King Justice only a grocery list the night he disappeared twelve years ago? Why has he come back, now? Yeah, those are just some of the questions I would've asked on any *other* night. But tonight, I had only one: "Can I go home now?"

"It's tough being a sidekick, isn't it?" The Strike asked.

Oh great. It was the worst night of my life and I was stuck listening to Chicken Noodle Soup for the Sidekick's Soul.

"You know, when I first became a superhero, I called myself The Brown Streak. It took me six months to figure out why all the villains kept laughing at me." He paused.

"What's your point?"

"I don't know. I thought there was a moral in there somewhere." The Strike thought for a moment. "Look, Speedy, after tonight, I know you want to give it all up and quit the Sidekicks . . ."

"Why shouldn't I? Or didn't you notice me eating a few mouthfuls of mud tonight? Or maybe you haven't seen me waxing the Pumpkin-mobile lately, or you were busy doing whatever it is that you do the last time I saved the world and Charisma Kid got all the credit! What's in all this for me?!"

"Just hang in there," The Strike said.

"'Hang in there'?" I echoed. I couldn't believe it. This guy was starting to sound like my dad! "*That's* your advice? *That's* why you brought me up here?"

"Look, I'm better at punching evil in the face than giving words of wisdom, okay? But yeah, that's it. Hang in there," The Strike repeated. "You've got a wonderful future ahead of you. A wonderful future . . ."

And with that, as he had done so many times before, The Strike shot into the sky and disappeared like a puff of smoke in the wind.

"HEY! HEY!" I shouted as loudly as I could. "WHO ARE YOU?!" But it was too late. He was gone. And then I remembered an even more important question . . .

"HOW THE HECK AM I GONNA GET DOWN FROM HERE?!"

Epilogue I
The First Epilogue!

The next day, I was back at the League of Big Justice. A few minutes after The Strike had zoomed into the sky, my dad drove up in his car. He called the fire department, and they helped me get down from the bridge support.

I wandered through the League of Big Justice Super Justice Lobby until I came to King Justice's Happy Place of Thinking and Satellite TV. The door slid open before I even knocked. King Justice waited inside.

"Speedy! Enter, my accelerating pal, and answer me this!" he rose from his favorite lounge chair and pointed to his large TV screen. "Will they vote Jim off the island? Will they vote Amy off the island? Only! Time! Will! Tell!"

"I'm sorry to bother you, sir . . ."

"Nonsense! Enter and bask in the glow of congratulations as I shake the five knuckles of justice in your honor!" King Justice rose his fist and . . . shook his five knuckles of justice in my honor. "Take that, evil!" He lowered his hand and patted me on the back. "I offer you thanks and gratitude! Pumpkin Pete has told me that without you, he would have never been able to defeat the crazy caramel corn ways of The Candy Man!"

"So . . . so he really told you what I did?" I couldn't believe it! Pete finally gave me credit!

"Yes! He told me how you cheered and rooted as he flossed The Candy Man into submission!" King Justice put a massive hand on my back. "Never underestimate the value of having someone believe in you. Siss! Boom! Ba!"

I shook my head in dismay. When will I learn?

"And now, my express mail human, allow me to wrap you in the fluffy down pillow of inquest!"

"Uh . . . you want to ask me a question?"

"Do I! Would it be possible for you to do me the greatest favor one hero has asked another?"

This was so awesome! Maybe he heard what Charisma Kid did to me at the football game and

King Justice was going to ask me to be his new sidekick! Or better yet, maybe he was going to ask me to join the League of Big Justice!

"By all that's Spandex! Save me from the mad moppet known only as . . . Super! Vision! Lad!"

As the words left King Justice's mouth, Super Vision Lad bolted out from behind the couch. He raced over to King Justice and started punching him in the knee.

"Big man go punch!" Super Vision Lad shouted. "Yaaaay!"

"The world has never known a greater threat!" King Justice claimed.

"But Super Vision Lad's not a villain!" I replied.

"Villain! No! Pain in the neck! Yes! And! Such! Torture! For only ten dollars per hour!" King Justice gently nudged Super Vision Lad toward me.

"Don't dwink shampoo!" Super Vision Lad yelled.

I took Super Vision Lad's hand and was about to leave when I remembered the reason I came. I turned to King Justice and said, "Thanks for giving me the chance to a be a sidekick. I won't let you down."

King Justice smiled, and Super Vision Lad bit my arm.

Epilogue II
The Last Epilogue!

I led Super Vision Lad into the Sidekick Super Clubhouse. Boom Boy was there with Spelling Beatrice. Cake and candy covered our table.

"CANDYYY!" Super Vision Lad shouted. He broke from my grip and raced to the table.

"Hey! Hey!" Boom Boy said. "You missed all the fun yesterday!"

"Yeah. I was a little busy saving the world from The Candy Man," I informed him.

"Hey! More hamburgers for me!" Boom Boy replied.

"Where'd all the candy and cake come from?" I asked.

"Oh, we took it out of the pockets of that nut you glued yourself to yesterday."

Before I could say anything about what a bad idea that was, Exact Change Kid came into the room with someone who appeared to be a new sidekick. The main reason I thought that is because we're the only ones stupid enough to wear Spandex when it isn't Halloween.

"Who's that?" I asked Boom Boy.

"That's the new sidekick — Haiku Boy. We think he's gonna be a boomtastic addition to the team!"

Haiku Boy walked over to me and said, "Red cherry blossoms. Fall upon silent waters. Punching evil's face."

"What?" I said.

"Frogs hop on green stones. Flowers bend to kiss the sun. You look so confused."

"Do you always speak in haiku?" I asked.

"The ocean waves come. Fish glisten in the morning. I speak just haiku." Haiku Boy smiled.

"So . . . he's going to fight evil with poetry?" I asked Exact Change Kid.

"Not just poetry," Exact Change Kid proudly announced. "Japanese poetry in lines of five, seven, and five syllables!"

I stared at Haiku Boy. He wore a bright red

Spandex uniform. On his chest were the Japanese characters for "haiku." Either that, or they were just some crazy scribbles that he thought all of us would *think* said "haiku." His hair was spiky and blue, like he just fell out of a bad anime cartoon. He was constantly shifting into dramatic action poses, as if evil would attack at any second. He also wore red sports goggles.

"A gray mist lingers! The moon hangs low in the sky! Haiku Boy chops evil!" He gave a few quick karate chops to the air.

"Uh . . . you know that last line was six syllables?" I asked.

"Dude! Are you telling Haiku Boy how to haiku?" Boom Boy laughed. "That's like telling you how to run fast."

"No, listen," I said, counting on my fingers to demonstrate. "Hai-ku Boy chops e-vil. Six syllables."

"Ohhh!" Boom Boy replied. "So *that's* what a syllable is!"

I could see beads of sweat rolling down the side of Haiku Boy's face. "I . . . I guess that's why I'm just a *sidekick*." He sighed. "I guess I'm not very good yet. . . ."

"Don't worry about it," I assured him. "All of us still have problems with our powers."

"But how many of you recite six syllables instead of five for the last line of a haiku?" Haiku Boy hung his head. "None of you. *That's* how many."

"Aw, so you can't count right," Boom Boy stepped in. "You've got a home now with the Sidekicks. We're a team, and we always work together to help each other out. So don't worry. If you make a mistake, we're here to catch you, buddy!"

"Wow. That's so cool." Haiku Boy cheered up. "I know this is the beginning of a great superhero career!" He put out his hand. "By the way, my name's Ivan Williams."

Exact Change Kid's eyes widened. Boom Boy shook his head. He leaned toward me and whispered, "Do you want to tell him he's kicked out of the Sidekicks for breaking Rule #1, or should I?"

Author Bios
Biographies of the Authors!

Dan Danko attributes his love of comic books to his childhood belief that he's from another planet. To this day, he has yet to be proven wrong.

Dan lists one of his greatest accomplishments as being fluent enough in Japanese to speak to a dim-witted seven-year-old. If Dan isn't watching Lakers' games, you'll find him traveling to any country that has a traveler's advisory from the U.S. State Department — much to his mother's dismay.

He's the tall one.

Tom Mason's love of comic books and all things superhero-y began when he had the flu and his parents bought him a stack of comics and sent him to the doctor.

When he's not selling his family's heirlooms on eBay or scuba diving off the California coast, he enjoys playing horseshoes with a long list of celebrities, all of whom once appeared on *The Love Boat*.

He's the cute one.

Dan and **Tom** are former editors and writers for Malibu and Marvel Comics, and they have also written for the TV series *Malcolm in the Middle* and *Rugrats*. They've been story editors on *Pet Alien* and on Nickelodeon's *Brothers Flub*.

Their combined height is twelve feet, one inch.

P.S. And they still read comic books!